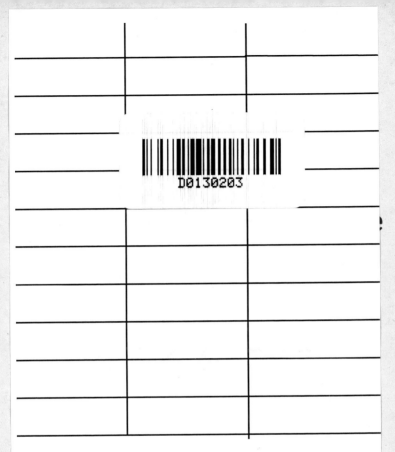

D0130203

Please return this book on or before the date shown above. To renew go to www.essex.gov.uk/libraries, ring 0345 603 7628 or go to any Essex library.

Essex County Council

Other titles by Holly Webb

Lost in the Snow

Alfie all Alone

Lost in the Storm

Sam the Stolen Puppy

Max the Missing Puppy

Sky the Unwanted Kitten

Timmy in Trouble

Ginger the Stray Kitten

Harry the Homeless Puppy

Buttons the Runaway Puppy

Alone in the Night

Ellie the Homesick Puppy

Jess the Lonely Puppy

Misty the Abandoned Kitten

Oscar's Lonely Christmas

Lucy the Poorly Puppy

Smudge the Stolen Kitten

The Rescued Puppy

The Kitten Nobody Wanted

The Lost Puppy

The Frightened Kitten

The Secret Puppy

The Abandoned Puppy

The Missing Kitten

The Puppy who was Left Behind

The Kidnapped Kitten

The Scruffy Puppy

The Brave Kitten

The Forgotten Puppy

The Secret Kitten

A Home for Molly

Sammy the Shy Kitten

The Seaside Puppy

The Curious Kitten

Monty the Sad Puppy

The Homeless Kitten

A Kitten Called Tiger

The Unwanted Puppy

The Rescued Kitten

The Shelter Puppy

The Perfect Kitten

The Puppy Who Couldn't Sleep

The Loneliest Kitten

The Mystery Kitten

The Story Puppy

The Saddest Kitten

The Kitten Next Door

The Puppy Who Ran Away

Nadia and the Forever Kitten

Holly Webb

Illustrated by Sophy Williams

LiTTLE TiGER

LONDON

This book was inspired by my cat Star!

STRIPES PUBLISHING LIMITED
An imprint of the Little Tiger Group
1 Coda Studios, 189 Munster Road, London SW6 6AW

Imported into the EEA by Penguin Random House Ireland,
Morrison Chambers, 32 Nassau Street, Dublin D02 YH68

A paperback original
First published in Great Britain in 2021

Text copyright © Holly Webb, 2021
Illustrations copyright © Sophy Williams, 2021
Author photograph © Charlotte Knee Photography

ISBN: 978-1-78895-304-7

A CIP catalogue record for this book is available from the British Library.

Printed and bound in the UK.

The Forest Stewardship Council® (FSC®) is a global, not-for-profit
organization dedicated to the promotion of responsible forest management
worldwide. FSC defines standards based on agreed principles for
responsible forest stewardship that are supported by environmental, social,
and economic stakeholders. To learn more, visit www.fsc.org

10 9 8 7 6 5 4 3 2 1

Chapter One

"I can't believe we'll be in Year Six next year," Nadia said, as she and Violet gathered up the pens and pencils and odd bits out of their classroom drawers. It was the last day of school before the summer holidays and they had to tidy everything up before the final assembly.

"I know!" Violet shook her head.

"We'll be the oldest when we come back in September. Oh, I can't wait for the holidays. Are you going away?"

Nadia sighed. "No. Not this summer. My dad's given up his job, to start a business by himself. He's got to work really hard and we can't afford a holiday. Mum said we'll have some fun days out instead, though. Go to London for the day, maybe. What about you?"

"I'm going to stay with my dad in August," Violet said. "But my mum's too busy working at the shelter for us to go away. Summer means kitten time. We've already got loads to look after!"

Violet's mum Michelle worked for a charity that rescued stray cats and Violet got to help out in the holidays. Her mum brought a lot of her work home…

Nadia gave her an envious look. "Lucky!"

"I know." Violet smiled. "They're really cute. Mum's a bit worried though, she says we're running out of space. If more cats turn up, we won't have anywhere to put them. We've already got kittens in our bathroom."

"That sounds so cool. Can I come and see them?"

"Course you can. Actually you can *have* them… It's really tricky if you get up to go to the loo in the middle of the night!"

"Violet!" Nadia giggled.

"It is!" But Violet started laughing too.

Two days later, Nadia went round to Violet's house to see the kittens. Violet had told her they were just starting to stumble around, like three little furry balloons with legs. They were named Trevor, Tilly and Tim.

"What happened to their mum?"

Nadia asked. She was sitting on the bathroom floor with Trevor, a tiny black kitten, slumped asleep in her lap.

"We don't know," Violet said sadly. "Mum said they were found in a box by some bins. Someone heard them squeaking and brought them to the shelter. We have to bottle-feed them. Even in the middle of the night!"

Nadia sighed at the thought. The kittens were so lovely – she wouldn't mind waking up to do that. She ran her finger over Trevor's dusty black fur and he shivered and twitched in his sleep.

"You can help feed them now," Violet suggested. "They're going to wake up starving any second." Almost as soon as she had said it, Tim, the black-and-white kitten draped over her leg, opened his dark blue eyes and started to make bossy little squeaking noises.

"Are you sure?" Nadia said eagerly. "I don't want to get it wrong."

Violet grinned. "They won't let you. They're little milk-monsters. You just hold the bottle and watch them go."

Violet was right. As soon as the kittens saw Michelle arrive with their bottles, there was no stopping them. They erupted into even more pleading squeaks, begging to go first.

"Oh, you're so greedy," Michelle murmured, laughing as Tilly pawed at her legs, trying to reach the bottle. "It's OK, look, there's enough for everyone." She handed a bottle to Nadia. "Do you want to feed Trevor?"

Nadia nodded and then giggled as three kittens suddenly surged towards her. She held the bottle up to Trevor's mouth and the tiny kitten lunged at it. She laughed as he made slurping noises around the rubber teat.

After he'd finished, Trevor stretched out along Nadia's jeans, purring in a very smug, satisfied way.

"He's so gorgeous," Nadia murmured. "But isn't it hard, spending all this time with them and then having to give them to someone else?"

Violet had already explained that they only kept the kittens while they needed round-the-clock care – then they went back to the shelter to be adopted into their forever homes.

Violet tickled Tim behind the ears and looked thoughtful. "I guess I'm used to it. I mean, of course it's sad to say goodbye, but then I think of them having lovely homes, where they're bossing everyone around and being super spoiled."

Her mother laughed. "The new owners send me photos sometimes. It's really nice to see the kittens I knew as big, grown-up cats."

Violet nodded. "She puts them up round the shelter and it makes me feel so proud. It's like – we were part of that!"

"It would be special…" Nadia agreed, looking thoughtful. She imagined how good it would feel to help a kitten like Trevor find their forever home.

Violet nudged her. "If you're going to be home all summer, you could look after some kittens, you know. At your house. You're always looking for fosterers, aren't you, Mum?"

"Always." Michelle sighed. "I didn't tell you, I had a call this morning from an old lady who's found a feral cat in her garden. She thinks she's pregnant. I'm going round tomorrow to see if I can catch her." The doorbell sounded and Michelle got up. "I expect that's your mum, Nadia, I'll go and let her in."

"Do you think your mum and dad would let you?" Violet whispered, as her mum headed downstairs.

"I don't know… I've always wanted a cat and maybe now Dad's going to be working from home…" Nadia gave Violet a hopeful look. "It must be worth a try!"

There was a gentle knock at the bathroom door. "Have you got all those kittens safe?" Michelle called.

"All done!" Violet said.

Michelle opened the door carefully, explaining to Nadia's mum, "They're getting so adventurous now. They shoot out of the door so fast and I don't want them falling down the stairs!"

Nadia waved at her mum, who was

standing behind Michelle looking curious.

"Mum, this is Trevor. Isn't he gorgeous?"

"Oh, he is very sweet," her mum said, leaning down to look at the kitten climbing Nadia's T-shirt. She smiled at Michelle. "I can't believe you have a bathroom full of kittens!"

Michelle sighed. "Tell me about it. We haven't got staff at the shelter through the night, you see, and these little ones need feeding at all hours, so we try to foster them out. We're running out of fosterers, though. There are so many kittens being born right now – and it's the summer holidays so lots of our fosterers are going away."

"Mum…" Nadia started to say, and her mum laughed.

"I bet I know what you're going to ask!" she said.

"Well, couldn't we?" Nadia pleaded. "It was so much fun feeding Trevor."

"I'm not sure you'd think it was fun in the middle of the night," her mum said gently. "Your dad may be at home, Nadia, but I still have to get up and go to work. I'm not sure I can cope with kitten feeds at three in the morning, or whenever!" She smiled apologetically at Michelle. "Though they are beautiful… Hello, sweetheart…" She was talking to Tilly, who was investigating the laces on her trainers. She crouched down to tickle her under the chin and then laughed when Tilly erupted in a wild purr.

"I know what you mean about night-time feeds," Michelle said, shuddering. "It's exhausting. And don't worry, I'm not about to send you home with kittens! Although…" She paused, looking thoughtfully at Nadia's mum. "It isn't only orphaned kittens we look after. We do have older cats who need fostering sometimes. I was just telling the girls I had a call about a pregnant stray this morning. She needs a quiet place with no other cats around for giving birth. And when the kittens are born, she'll feed them herself. Worth considering, if you did want to help out. Just give me a call if you'd like to try."

Nadia fixed her mum with a hopeful stare. A mother cat and the tiniest possible kittens, in their house! "We're not going away," she reminded her. "I wouldn't mind if we didn't go on day trips."

"It's definitely something to think about,"

her mum said slowly. "But we'll have to talk to your dad first. He's the one who's going to be at home most of the time with you and a cat."

"And gorgeous kittens," Nadia added.

"Yes, and very sweet kittens," her mum agreed, laughing at Tilly, who was on her back fighting a battle to the death with a shoelace. "I promise we'll think about it, Nadia. We'll properly think about it."

Chapter Two

Nadia tried so hard not to pester Mum about Michelle's idea on the way home, but she couldn't get it out of her head.

"You're very quiet," her mum said, as they walked along their road.

Nadia looked up and saw that her mum was smiling. She must have figured out exactly what Nadia was thinking.

"I didn't want to go on about it, Mum," she said. "But I can't think of anything else!" She couldn't stop herself bouncing a little bit as she walked. "Just think! A cat! In our house! And kittens!"

"But not a cat we can keep," her mum pointed out. "It would only be for a while, Nadia. Wouldn't you miss her when she's gone? And the little kittens? I think it might be hard to say goodbye."

Nadia nodded. "I asked Violet about that. She said she's used to it and it would be harder for us. But knowing that we'll be helping the kittens find forever homes would make it easier. And Michelle says they really do need the help. I think that would make it worth being sad when we say goodbye. Don't you?"

Mum nodded and Nadia thought she looked a bit surprised. "Yes…" She leaned down and put her arm round Nadia's shoulders for a quick hug. "You're such a good girl sometimes."

Nadia crossed her fingers behind her back, feeling hopeful. But what was her dad going to say?

Afterwards, Nadia wondered if it was down to how cute Tilly had been, playing with Mum's shoelaces. Or maybe it was because Dad was feeling happy about a good day at work. Whatever the reason, her mum called Michelle later that evening to say yes,

they would foster the pregnant cat
– the old lady had called her Gracie.
Michelle was going round to collect
her in the morning and take her for a
check-up at the vet.

The following day, Nadia got up
early and put away all the washing-up
that had been left
on the draining
board overnight.
Then she
plugged in the
vacuum cleaner
and started hoovering
the living room.
When her mum
came downstairs,
she looked
confused.

"Nadia, what are you doing?"

Nadia glanced round. "I'm tidying up for Gracie."

"I don't think she's going to notice if the carpet's dusty…" Her mum smiled. "But it's very nice of you. I'll go and put some toast on."

By eleven, when Michelle was due to arrive with Gracie, Nadia was in the middle of cleaning her bedroom. She wanted everything to be perfect – *and* she was too excited to sit still. When the doorbell rang, she raced down the stairs in three jumps. She forced herself not to fling the front door wide open – Michelle had told Mum on the phone that Gracie would be really nervous, because she was a feral cat and she was about to have kittens. They would have to be quiet and gentle around her.

"Hi!" she whispered to Michelle and she beamed at Violet, who was standing beside her mum, with a squishy cat bed, a bag of food and all sorts of other bits in her arms. Michelle was carrying a plastic box with a wire front and Nadia could see a furry face looking back at her from inside.

"Hi, Michelle, hello, Violet!" Nadia's mum hurried out from the kitchen and her dad came down from his office. "Come on in. Shall we take her upstairs? We were going to put her in the spare room."

"That sounds great," Michelle said, and they all followed Nadia's dad up. Michelle carefully put the carrier down on the floor. "Hopefully we've brought everything you'll need."

"There's so much," Nadia murmured. She was carrying some of Violet's big pile now – food bowls and a bag of cat litter, and what looked like a couple of cat toys.

"Can we fill up the litter tray and her water bowl, maybe put a little dry food down to cheer her up?" Michelle suggested. "Then we'll see if she wants to come out. She might take a while, she's very shy. She's been living in an old lady's garden until now – apparently she let Mrs Jackson stroke her occasionally, but she never came into the house."

Nadia looked round from filling up the litter tray, eyeing the cat carrier hopefully. It sounded as though Gracie might be almost friendly, if she didn't mind being stroked.

Michelle unlatched the wire door of the carrier and stepped back. "Hey, Gracie," she said gently. "Want to come and see your new place?"

There was a rustle inside the carrier and then a suspicious nose appeared at the wire door, followed by some whiskers. Nadia guessed that Gracie was sniffing the air, trying to work out where she'd ended up. It must all seem very strange to her.

No sooner than they'd appeared, the whisker-tips shrank back inside the carrier and Michelle sighed. "Don't worry. I think Gracie just needs time to get used to the idea. I'm sure she'll come out soon. Thanks so much for clearing a room for her – this is perfect."

Nadia's mum and dad led Michelle and Violet downstairs for a cup of tea, but Nadia couldn't help lingering as her mum closed the door, peering round for one last look.

Usually in the holidays, Nadia went to a holiday club, at least for some of the time, but now that Dad was working from home, she didn't have to. She was enjoying being able to sleep in a bit later. It made Monday mornings a lot nicer. She stretched lazily, yawned and rolled over to see what time it was. It definitely felt like breakfast time. She would have a quick look round the door of Gracie's room too, on the way downstairs.

But as Nadia reached for her alarm clock, she froze, staring at the open wardrobe in the corner of her room.

There, lying on her shoes, was a small, stripey cat, glaring back at her.

Nadia swallowed. "Um… You're not supposed to be there," she whispered to Gracie. "You've got your own room…" She was almost sure Gracie was scowling, but maybe it was just the black M-shape of stripes above her eyes. Nadia slipped out of bed and scurried downstairs to find her mum and dad.

"Gracie's in my wardrobe!" she squeaked to her mum, who was making a cup of tea before she went to work.

"What?" Mum stared at her. "How? She was in the spare room!"

"Not any more." Nadia shook her head. "I just woke up and there she was, staring at me!"

Dad looked guilty. "I fed her when I got up… Maybe I didn't shut the door properly?"

They all hurried back upstairs to look at Gracie, who was still snuggled comfortably amongst Nadia's things.

"She looks ever so happy there," Dad murmured.

"Michelle said that when the kittens were close to coming, she'd want to make nests," Nadia remembered. "That's why they brought those fleecy blankets. Maybe she's about to have her kittens! Do you think she's nesting in my wardrobe?"

"Maybe," Mum said. "But I don't know if we ought to let her!"

"I can shut my bedroom door, so she doesn't go into the rest of the house," Nadia suggested. "She can't mind me being in here, since she came in while I was asleep!" She smiled at Gracie, and

Gracie glared back, and then yawned and stretched. Her tummy was looking very round, Nadia thought. Soon there would be kittens in her bedroom.

Later that week, Nadia and her mum were at Nadia's nani's house. Nani loved cats and Nadia was desperate to tell her all about Gracie.

"So do you know when the kittens are coming?" Nani asked hopefully.

"Soon, we think," Mum said.

Nadia sighed. "I was hoping she'd have had them by now. She made her nest in my wardrobe on Monday and now it's Thursday. Michelle said she thought Gracie was due any day!"

Nani chuckled. "Maybe she likes keeping you guessing. She's obviously got a mind of her own."

"I think she has," Mum agreed. "Actually, we ought to get back to check on her now, Nadia. Dad went out for that meeting, so Gracie's been on her own for a couple of hours. We'll see you soon, Mama."

Nadia gave Nani a hug. "We'll call

and tell you when she has the kittens," she promised. "You can come and see them!"

"I'd love that," Nani said. "I still miss my Milo…"

"Aw, Nani." Nadia hugged her again harder. She'd loved fussing over Nani's cat Milo when they visited. He had been a huge white long-haired cat, definitely the biggest cat Nadia had ever seen. He had been three times the size of Gracie. "Me too. He was so friendly. I'd better go. See you soon!"

As they walked home, Nadia began to worry. "Do you think there might be something wrong with Gracie?" she asked her mum. "Maybe we should take her to the vet."

Mum frowned. "Michelle told us

they didn't know exactly when Gracie was due. Just soon. I'm sure it's OK, Nadia."

"I suppose." Nadia sighed. But it seemed they'd already waited so long. She was desperate to meet Gracie's kittens.

Dad was just arriving back when they got home, so Nadia hurried upstairs to look in on Gracie while her mum and dad chatted in the kitchen. The tabby cat was definitely friendlier than she had been when she first arrived. She still looked a bit suspicious whenever Nadia walked in (which Nadia thought was a bit unfair, really, since it was *her* bedroom) but then she seemed to relax. She didn't mind if Nadia sat close by on her beanbag and read a book, or lay on the floor and drew. Nadia had drawn a lot of cats…

Nadia opened the door quietly, still trying hard not to scare Gracie. "Hey," she whispered as she tiptoed in. "My nani's really excited about you— Oh! Gracie!" Nadia stopped in the middle of her bedroom, gazing wide-eyed at her wardrobe.

Gracie was stretched out on her side and next to her were five tiny bundles of fur.

Chapter Three

Nadia closed the door very quietly and stood on the other side of it for a moment, her eyes huge and round, her heart thumping. Her wardrobe was full of kittens! Then she raced to find her parents.

"Mum! Dad! She's had them! Gracie had the kittens while we were at Nani's!" she yelled from halfway down the stairs, and her mum and dad both came out into the hallway looking shocked.

"Is she OK?" Dad asked.

"I didn't look for very long," Nadia admitted. "I was so surprised, I just came to tell you. But I think so. They were all lying next to her, I think they were feeding."

"We were supposed to ring Michelle when Gracie started giving birth!" Mum said, her face worried. "Let's take a quick look, then I'll give her a call."

They padded softly back up the stairs, whispery and excited, and peered round Nadia's door. Gracie lifted her head wearily to watch them, but she didn't seem too bothered that they were there.

"They look OK, don't they?" Nadia murmured. "I love the way they're lined up!" The kittens were all feeding, in a neat little row.

"They're so different," Mum said.

Nadia nodded. She had assumed that all the kittens would look just like Gracie, but although there were two perfect tabbies, there were also two soft, smoky-grey kittens and one tiny ginger one, with long white boots and a white front. Nadia hadn't really been ready for how small the kittens would be either – like furry beanbags, with stubby pink paws poking out. Their eyes were closed, and they nuzzled and squeaked and squirmed up against Gracie.

"Can I stay in here?" Nadia asked quietly. "I just want to look at the kittens for a bit. Do you think Gracie will mind?"

Nadia's mum put her hand over her mouth to muffle a laugh. "I think she might be too tired to care, Nadia. I'll ring Michelle, she'll want to come round and make sure they're all healthy."

"I'll stay and watch with you," Dad said, sitting on the end of Nadia's bed so he could see inside the wardrobe. "I've never seen such tiny kittens. And she managed it all by herself, without us even knowing about it. You're a star, Gracie…"

The smallest of the kittens stretched
out her paws blindly, squeaking
for milk. She was so hungry. She
twisted her head around, trying to
find somewhere to suck. One of the
big grey kittens blundered into her,
accidentally pushing her out of the
way – he was hungry too and he
didn't even notice that he'd shoved his
little sister.

The little ginger kitten mewed and wriggled, sniffing the air for the smell of milk. She waved her paws, still cheeping for attention, and then her mother leaned over and nudged her close, nuzzling her up against the other kittens. The ginger kitten squeaked, catching the scent of milk, and latched on at last. But she was so tired and it was hard work suckling. She drank a little and dozed, then drank a little more.

The big grey kitten scrambled closer, eager for milk, and bumped his tiny sister again. She gave a faint mew of surprise, then she curled herself away from his nudging paws and drifted back to sleep...

When her mum and dad agreed to look after Gracie, Nadia had never dreamed that she'd end up with five kittens in her bedroom – but she wasn't complaining, even though the kittens' little squeaks and mumbles often woke her up in the night. Even Violet had never had a bedroom full of kittens and she was quite jealous when she finally got to meet them a few days later.

"You've got kittens in your bathroom!" Nadia pointed out.

"And the kitchen now too." Violet sighed. "Mum said she couldn't turn the last lot away. There are kittens *everywhere*. But I'd love them in my bedroom. Yours are so sweet, especially the plushy grey ones."

The grey kittens were beautiful, but

Nadia thought the tiny ginger one was the sweetest. She always seemed to be at the bottom of the kitten pile, being stomped on by her brothers and sisters. She was much smaller than the others too.

Nadia and her mum and dad had been talking about names for the kittens – Nadia had decided that Luna suited the ginger kitten. The white patch under her chin was almost a perfect circle, like a full moon. Mum wanted to call the two grey kittens Jo and Jem, and the tabbies were Ani and Arya.

"I wonder what colour their eyes will be," Nadia said, smiling as Jo – or at least, she thought it was Jo – scrambled over the pile of kittens and slumped on to Gracie's back for a sleep. Gracie looked a bit surprised.

"They won't open for about a week, but they'll all have blue eyes to start with," Violet said. "Then they'll change when they're a couple of weeks old."

"I never knew that!"

"Their ears are closed up when they're born too," Violet told her. "They're probably only starting to hear now."

Just then Michelle came in with Nadia's parents – they'd been having a cup of tea downstairs. She kneeled on the floor a little way from the wardrobe and looked thoughtfully at Gracie and the kittens. "She looks very proud of herself," she said, smiling.

"Do you think the kittens are OK?" Nadia asked anxiously.

"They look fine." Michelle leaned a little closer, trying not to upset Gracie. Then she glanced back at Nadia. "Why? Are you worried about them?"

Nadia shrugged. Michelle knew so much about cats and so did Violet. She didn't want to say something stupid. But she *was* worried… "It's just … the little ginger one. She's smaller than the others and I don't think she's having as much milk as they are. It's like she's too sleepy to bother feeding for long." She smiled shyly at Michelle. "I've been watching them a lot."

Michelle nodded. "That's really useful to know, Nadia. Well done. She's definitely looking a bit small and she's not moving around as much as the other kittens either."

Nadia didn't know whether to be
pleased or not. She was glad
she'd been right, but
she didn't want Luna
to have something
wrong with her.
"Will she be
OK?" she asked,
crouching down
next to Michelle.
Luna was curled
up on her own, a
little way off from
the other kittens.

"I think she just needs
more food," Michelle said thoughtfully.

"Gracie has tried to get her to feed,"
Nadia said. "I saw her picking Luna
up in her mouth! She was trying to get

her closer. But the other kittens have started wriggling about now and they squish her…"

Michelle nodded. "I know. They don't mean to, but it's easy for the weakest kitten to get pushed out. I think Luna – is that what you're calling her? I think she might need some help." She smiled at Nadia. "Remember how good you were at feeding Trevor?"

"Oh!" Nadia reached out excitedly to grab Violet's hand and squeeze it. "But… Luna's so little. Although I suppose Trevor and Tilly and Tim were that size too, when you started."

"Exactly." Michelle looked at Nadia's mum and dad. "Do you think you'll be able to do it? It looks like Luna's still getting some milk from Gracie, so we just need to top her up. But it will mean feeding her every couple of hours – though you can probably get away with every four hours during the night."

Nadia's dad looked worriedly at her mum.

"It's a lot, I know," Michelle said. "I can try to find a more experienced foster home if this is going to be too much. I did say Gracie would feed the kittens herself!"

There was a moment of silence and Nadia glanced anxiously from her mum to her dad. Every two hours was a big ask.

"Well … it's your bedroom, Nadia," Dad said slowly. "I'm guessing Gracie won't want us to move her back to the spare room."

"I don't mind!" Nadia said quickly.

"I honestly can't imagine sending them somewhere else." Dad shrugged. "I've got used to popping in to check on them every time I stop for a cup of tea. Gracie's such a good mum – she just needs a bit of help with Luna. She's a lot less jumpy as well. I think she's starting to trust us."

Mum laughed. "I was expecting it to be Nadia who fell in love with them, not you!"

Dad put his arm round Nadia. "Me and Nadia both, I think."

Chapter Four

"Your eyes are opening!"

Luna blinked muzzily up at the voice above her. She knew that voice, the softer, lighter one. The girl, the one who fed her.

"They're blue, just like Violet said they would be," Nadia murmured as she gently stroked Luna's head. "That's so exciting, Luna. You can see me! At least, you'll be able to soon. I suppose you don't really understand what's happening right now."

Luna wriggled and let out a tiny, wailing squeak, hoping for milk. Where was the bottle? She could *smell* milk… She tried to focus on the girl, on Nadia, leaning over her, but all she could really see was shapes and shadows. She padded her paws frantically against the soft cat bed, blundering towards Nadia, and food.

"It's OK, here you go, look…" Luna felt herself lifted gently on to a soft towel and then the teat of the bottle brushed against her mouth. She sucked at it eagerly, spluttering milk all round her face to start with and then settling to a slow, steady gulp.

"You're getting so good at this now. I'm sure I can see you growing, Luna... There, you've nearly finished it."

Luna slurped happily at the last few drops in the bottle and then slumped back on to the towel in a milky daze. She shivered a little as Nadia gently wiped her face and then stroked along her back. She let out a tiny purr, arching into the soft fingers, and she heard Nadia laugh. Then Luna felt herself lifted again, cupped carefully in Nadia's hands, and then laid down alongside her mother.

53

She twitched her ears as Gracie began to lick her clean and snuggled in closer to the softly breathing pile of kittens.

"Oh, Nadia. They're getting so big! Are you still bottle-feeding the little ginger one?" Nani sat down on the edge of Nadia's bed and peered admiringly at the kittens.

"Yes, but we won't have to for much longer, Michelle said. They're three weeks old, so we can start giving them kitten food soon. We have to mix it up with milk – it's going to be so messy."

"That's good. You wouldn't want to be up in the night feeding her once you're back at school."

Nadia made a face. "It's ages till I go back to school, though. We're only halfway through the summer holidays." Halfway… She couldn't imagine going back to school and not spending all day with Gracie and the kittens.

"You've done so well feeding her," Nani said. "I called her the little one, but she's nearly as big as the others now."

"She is," Nadia said proudly. She looked down at Luna, who was curled comfortably in her lap, and smiled. Luna's ginger fur was looking thick and fluffy, and her white boots shone – all those bottles of milk were working. "She's not quite as brave as the others, though. They love exploring my bedroom and they get everywhere."

"I can see," Nani said, laughing as Jo started to climb up her trousers. "Ooooh! I'm glad I've got churidar on, Nadia, he's digging his claws in!"

Nadia gently unhooked the grey kitten and popped him back in the cat bed next to Gracie. "He won't be there for long," she said, shaking her head. "He's the most adventurous of them all."

Jo might be the bravest, but Nadia thought that Luna was the sweetest of the kittens – maybe it was because she'd been hand-feeding her, and it made her seem special. But Luna did seem to love her back. She always came wobbling over to Nadia, whenever Nadia came into the room. She'd sit on her hind paws, batting at Nadia's legs and asking to be picked up. She always wanted to sleep on Nadia too – sometimes when she was really tired, Luna would just collapse on Nadia's feet, as if she didn't have the energy to climb any further. Even in the hot summer weather, Nadia thought there was nothing nicer than a tiny kitten slumped asleep on her foot.

Even though Nadia had been sure the summer would last for ages, the second half of the holidays seemed to flash by even faster than the first. All too soon, Nadia's dad was telling her to make sure her school bag was ready, and asking if she needed him to get her any more white socks.

The kittens were six weeks old now and eating solid food, although they still fed from Gracie too. Luna didn't really need Nadia to bottle-feed her any more, but she was still having one bottle a day – mostly because if she didn't get it, she would squeak and complain like anything, and Nadia just couldn't resist. Michelle had said it wouldn't do her any harm and Luna would grow out of milk soon anyway.

Now that the kittens were getting so much bigger, Michelle and the staff at the shelter were starting to think about new homes for them. The kittens had already been featured on the shelter's website as being available soon. Nadia didn't know whether to be pleased or sorry. She was so proud of her kittens, going off to grown-up homes – but she hated the thought of saying goodbye.

"I've had quite a few messages about the kittens," Michelle told Nadia and her dad, when they met at the school gates on the first morning back. "Especially the two grey ones. The tabbies too."

"Not little Luna?" Dad asked, sounding surprised.

"Not as much as the others," Michelle admitted.

Nadia frowned. Why wouldn't anyone want Luna?

"So would it be all right if a couple of people came to see them over the next week?" Michelle asked. "To see if they'd like to adopt one, once they're ready to leave Gracie?"

"I can't imagine them leaving her," Nadia murmured. "Gracie looks after them all so well. Especially Luna. It feels like she needs her mum…"

Michelle smiled. "Gracie's a very good mother. But she needs time to herself now too – we want her to start getting used to being away from the kittens, so she's ready for them to leave as well. You could let her explore a different room, maybe?"

Dad brightened up. "She can be in my office. I'd like the company, actually. She's much friendlier than she was when she first arrived."

Nadia chewed her bottom lip. Dad was right – Gracie seemed to enjoy being stroked now, if they picked the right moment. It seemed sad that she had to get used to being separated from her kittens, but maybe she'd like the peace and quiet. Nadia still didn't want to think about the kittens leaving her and Gracie behind.

"Oh, look, they're so sweet!"

Luna woke up with a jump. She'd been snoozing, snuggled up against her mother, but now there was someone strange and loud in the room. Luna was used to Nadia, and her mum and dad, and even Nani and Michelle and Violet, but this was someone different. She retreated behind Gracie, who was sitting up now, eyeing the visitor suspiciously.

"So the two tabby kittens are girls, the grey ones are a girl and a boy, and the ginger one — we call her Luna — she's a girl," Nadia's dad explained.

"I love the grey ones!" the woman exclaimed, crouching down next to the play pen that Nadia's dad had fixed across the front of the wardrobe.

Now that Nadia was back at school, they didn't want the kittens roaming around her bedroom, in case they hurt themselves or got trapped somewhere. Luna didn't mind the pen but Jo spent most of his time trying to mountaineer out of it. He was getting very good at climbing the mesh sides, he was halfway up there now.

"The ginger one looks a bit shy, doesn't she? Is it OK if I pick this lovely grey one up?" the woman asked, and Luna flinched further back, as she leaned right over the pen and reached for Jo.

From behind her mother, Luna watched Jo clambering across the woman's lap, sniffing and nuzzling at her. He didn't seem to be frightened of

her at all, not even when she laughed,
a high, loud noise that made Luna's
ears flatten. Her sisters were crowded
curiously at the front of the pen,
watching the woman cuddle Jo. They
patted the mesh with their paws and
mewed for their turn to be taken out,
to explore, to be petted. Luna just
wished Nadia was there.

Over the next few days, the same thing happened again and again. People came, strange people who wanted to fuss over the kittens and pick them up and cuddle them. No one seemed to want to lift Luna out of the pen, but she didn't mind. She was quite happy hidden away at the back. Happy and safe.

Chapter Five

Violet tickled Arya the tabby kitten under her chin, and laughed as she stuck her nose in the air and closed her eyes blissfully. Violet had come home with Nadia after school, and the two girls were sitting on Nadia's bedroom floor with Arya and Luna climbing all over them. "So she's going tomorrow?"

"Yes…" Nadia rubbed Arya's ears, and

she began to purr at the double love she was getting. "Then we'll only have Luna left." She made a face. Arya, Ani, Jo and Jem were all going to perfect forever homes. It seemed so unfair that Luna was left behind. "I don't understand people, I really don't. No one wanted to look at her! Just because she's a bit shy. She'd have gone to them if they hadn't been all loud and grabby."

Luna was curled in Nadia's lap in a tiny ginger ball. She kept getting up and looking around though, as if she just couldn't settle. Nadia wasn't sure if she was worried about the other kittens or she was looking for Gracie.

The kittens' mother was with Dad in his office – probably stretched out comfortably next to his computer keyboard, which seemed to be her new favourite place. Since Michelle had suggested it a couple of weeks ago, she'd been having time away from her kittens, but Nadia was sure Luna didn't like it.

"She'll find a home soon," Violet said. She was trying to be reassuring, but Nadia ducked her head, not wanting her friend to see her worried face. "I know she's shy, but someone's going to love her," Violet went on. "And lots of people really like ginger fur."

"Like me!" Nadia said, looking up indignantly. "How could anyone not like ginger fur? Luna's gorgeous! I love her white boots. And she's got the nicest little pink feet."

Violet laughed. "I know. I think she's beautiful too."

"You're a lovely colour," Nadia murmured comfortingly to Luna. "The prettiest of all the kittens and don't let anyone tell you different."

Luna peered uncertainly round the edge of Nadia's bedroom door into the hallway. Nadia had left for school a while ago and the house was quiet. Even though Luna was starting to get used to Nadia being away in the daytime, she still missed her, and she was a little bored without the other kittens to play with.

Gracie was curled up on the bed, dozing. Luna had learned how to climb up the edge of the duvet and scrabble her way on to the bed, but she didn't feel like snuggling up with her mum. The bedroom door was open and Luna was feeling adventurous. She was growing up and getting bolder, and now Nadia's dad had taken the pen away from the wardrobe, she wanted to explore her home properly.

Luna put her nose through the gap and then glanced back at Gracie on the bed. Her mother had one eye open, watching her. But that's all she was doing, just watching. It was all right then, Luna thought. She was allowed.

More confidently now, she padded out on to the landing and looked around. Then a little further… Luna turned to make sure the door was still there, and it was. She knew how to get back. Slowly, she walked along the landing, sniffing and nosing at the carpet, the cracks under the doors, a laundry basket – she scrabbled her paws at that curiously, but she didn't know what it was.

The other doors on the landing were shut, so she stood at the top of the stairs instead, staring down. They were so big! Gracie went down there sometimes, but Luna was sure she could never manage all those steps. She would have to wait for Nadia to carry her, she thought, then she could explore more. Luna slumped down with her chin on the carpet, her paws dangling over the top step, settling into a comfortable doze.

"Is Luna missing the other kittens?" Violet asked. She and Nadia were curled up on one of the playground benches, keeping an eye on a wild game of football that was getting a bit close.

"Maybe a little?" Nadia said thoughtfully. "She's doing a lot of exploring round the house. And she definitely wants me to play with her more." She smiled, remembering the tiny ginger kitten she'd found waiting for her at the top of the stairs the day before. "I love it. She's so funny, she plays with everything – even my hair!" She twitched the wavy end of her ponytail at Violet. "Gracie's almost started playing too," she added, looking proud. "Dad said she keeps stealing his pens and knocking them off the table on purpose. And then she stares at him until he picks them up so she can do it all over again!"

"Does he do it?" Violet asked.

"Every time! He really loves having her. I never expected him to like fostering so much. And the more Gracie gets used to living in a family, the more likely she is to be adopted. Don't you think?"

Violet nodded. "Once Luna's been adopted, Gracie can go back to the shelter. She's a lot less wild than she was, and she's beautiful. It might take a while for her to find a home, because she's so shy… But I'm sure someone's going to love her." Both the girls got up as the whistle went and wandered across the playground to the door.

Nadia was sure that Violet was right, but all afternoon she kept thinking about Gracie and Luna, and finding them their forever homes. *We're doing a good job,* she told herself, as she tried to listen to Miss Evans explaining their history project. *I really want Gracie and Luna to go to lovely people. I've been worrying for ages that no one wants Luna! And I know that when they do it'll be because we looked after them so well.* But she couldn't help thinking, *Won't Luna miss me when she goes to live somewhere else? I know I miss her, even when I'm at school. I can't imagine never seeing her again...*

Nadia chewed on the end of her pencil, forgetting about school entirely.

Maybe – maybe we could just keep her? And Gracie? Then they wouldn't have to be split up!

Nadia couldn't understand why she hadn't thought of it before, because now it seemed perfect. Except – they were only supposed to be fostering... Mum and Dad had never agreed to adopt a cat forever, certainly not a cat *and* a kitten. Nadia heaved a sigh that sent her worksheet halfway across the table and then hurriedly snatched it back, looking embarrassed.

"Are you all right, Nadia?" Miss Evans asked. "Are you stuck?"

"Er… No," Nadia said, staring down at her blank worksheet. "I'm all right. Sorry." She gritted her teeth and glared at the questions. There was only a tiny bit of the afternoon left and Mum was picking her up today. Perhaps she could talk to her about adopting Gracie and Luna on the way home.

But as she dashed out into the playground with Violet after school, she saw her mum and Michelle standing together in the crowd of parents. They didn't notice as she and Violet arrived, and Nadia saw Michelle pat her mum's arm.

"You don't know how grateful we are, Farida. We were really stuck and it's been so helpful having you look after Gracie and the kittens."

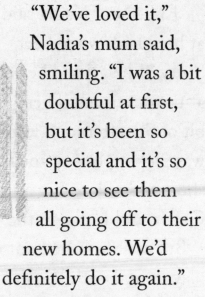

"We've loved it," Nadia's mum said, smiling. "I was a bit doubtful at first, but it's been so special and it's so nice to see them all going off to their new homes. We'd definitely do it again."

Michelle nodded eagerly. "Well, that won't be a problem – we always have cats that need a lovely foster home."

Nadia slowed to a walk, biting her lip.

How could she ask her mum to stop fostering, when there were so many other cats who needed their help?

Chapter Six

The next day, Luna peered up at her mother, who was stretched out along the desk above her. Every so often, Nadia's dad would stop typing and stroke her. If he didn't stroke her often enough, Gracie would roll over and tap his arm with her paw. She had him very well trained.

Dad didn't like Luna walking about

on his keyboard, though. She'd only
been trying to follow his fingers,
but he'd put her back down on the
floor. Luna patted at a pile of books
and papers instead, enjoying the
rustly noises they made. But it wasn't
enough to keep her occupied for long.
If Nadia were there, she would have
crumpled the paper into a ball and
thrown it about for her to chase, Luna
thought. Nadia was very good at that,
and Luna loved growling fiercely at
the scrunched-up paper and then
shredding it into bits with her tiny
claws.

Nadia wasn't going to be back for
a while though, Luna was fairly sure.
She'd have to find something else to
keep her busy. She padded across the

carpet and out on to the landing – she was planning to go back to Nadia's room; it was more interesting than Dad's office and she still wasn't sure about trying to climb down the stairs. Nadia's room had more things to chase and burrow under and play with – the office was too tidy.

But suddenly Luna pulled up short, her eyes wide and curious. There was another door, at the end of the landing. She'd seen the door before, of course, but she'd never seen it standing open, the way it was now. There was a faint, fresh smell floating out and a fascinating sound of birdsong. Luna hurried along the landing to investigate and popped her head round the door.

Stretching up in front of her was a flight of steps and Luna eyed them sadly. Stairs, again! Why were there always stairs to stop her? She padded at the first step with one paw, catching the carpet fibres in her claws. The carpet was quite easy to grab on to, she noticed in surprise. Almost easier than Nadia's duvet. If she could climb up on to Nadia's bed, perhaps she could climb these steps? Luna stood up on her back paws and realized she could actually reach almost to the top of the step. If she jumped a little...

She dropped back, and then leaped and scrabbled mightily, finally landing on the first step with a triumphant twitch of her tail.

There were an awful lot more of those steps, though. Luna gazed upward for a moment and then set about grimly climbing again. She wanted to know what that scent was and she could feel a breeze ruffling her fur. On and on she clambered, until at last she slumped down on the very top step. She was almost too worn out to realize she had done it.

But the room was too interesting for Luna to be tired for long. She padded slowly across the floor, looking around at the furniture – particularly the bed, which had all sorts of interesting boxes and bags and shadowy spaces underneath. Luna poked her nose in and then reversed out quickly, sneezing at the dust.

She was still shaking her whiskers when she noticed a quiet buzzing over on the other side of the room. Intrigued, Luna hurried round the bed to look. Up above in the sloping ceiling was a window, a strange, angled window that tipped open to show a deep, calm blue sky. And crawling and bumbling around the bottom of the window was a fat, furry bee.

Luna was entranced. She had never seen a bumblebee before. She and Gracie had always been inside the house, and Nadia and Dad had been very careful not to open their windows, in case Luna or Gracie climbed out.

It was an effort after her hard climb up the stairs, but Luna scrambled up on to the bed to get closer to the frantic bee. It couldn't seem to work out how to get out of the gap again and it kept bumping into the glass.

All Luna's hunting instincts were roused now. She was desperate to get closer. She perched on the very edge of the bed, her bottom wiggling as she measured the jump to the shelving unit under the window. If she could make it there, she would be so close! Just as she sprang, the bee finally worked out what it was doing wrong and zoomed joyfully out into the sky. Luna landed on the top shelf of the unit a second later, slipping and scrabbling a little, but safe. Except there was no bee. She peered after it, feeling grumpy. All that hard work, climbing and jumping, and the furry buzzy thing had gone!

Still, even without the bee, the window was fascinating. Standing up on her back paws, Luna could poke her head out of the window quite easily. She'd spent ages sitting on Nadia's bedroom windowsill, watching the cars and the people in the street below, but this was much more exciting. The world was just out there for her to explore! She could hear birds calling and someone shouting in one of the gardens. And that delicious, strange breeze was making her want to sniff and climb and explore. It was definitely stronger than it had been before.

Luna's ears twitched curiously at a muffled bang from the bottom of the stairs. She peered round over her shoulder, but it was a noise she didn't recognize. She didn't know that it mattered, that the door to the stairs had swung shut behind her – the air outside was far more interesting. Luna wriggled out of the window and stood cautiously on the very edge of the frame.

She was on the roof!

"What's the matter?" Violet asked, nudging Nadia's arm gently. They were in an art lesson, building fossils out of papier mâché. Usually Nadia would have been up to her elbows in sticky newspaper, but she'd hardly touched her side of the ammonite at all.

Nadia looked at Violet for a moment. She wasn't sure what her friend was going to think… Then she sighed. "I just can't stop thinking about Luna and Gracie, that's all. No one seems to want to adopt Luna and I don't understand why! But I'm actually really glad because I don't want her to go! Or Gracie either."

"Oh…" Violet nodded thoughtfully.

"I think your mum might take Gracie and Luna back to the shelter soon, and give us another mother cat to foster," Nadia said in a small voice. She didn't want Violet to think she was criticizing her mum. "But … I wish we could just keep them…"

"You know, I bet my mum would be ever so pleased to find a good home for Gracie if you wanted to keep them both," Violet said.

"I can't stop thinking about it!" Nadia gave her a hopeful look. "You really think she would be OK with it? My dad loves Gracie so much too."

"Cats who've been wild for a long time are really hard to rehome. My mum said the other day she was a bit worried about Gracie. It's like she's somewhere in between a feral cat who wants to live outside and a pet cat who wants to be with a family."

"But your mum said how hard it was to find people to foster mother cats too." Nadia sighed. She'd been really proud they were doing such a special job, and she felt guilty about giving it up, even if it meant they got to keep Luna and Gracie. "She was so grateful to my mum, she said. We couldn't foster any more mothers if we had our own cats."

Violet nodded slowly. "That's true. But it sounds like Gracie's bonded with your dad – that's special. Mum ought to be throwing him a party!"

"It would be good to keep them together as well," Nadia said eagerly. "I think Luna really needs her mum. Even though we helped feed her, she and Gracie snuggle up together all the time, and Gracie's always washing Luna." She was silent for a minute, then she gave Violet a determined look. "You've made me feel better about it. I'm going to talk to Mum and Dad tonight. I'm going to tell them I think we have to keep Luna and Gracie. We just have to."

"I'd hug you if I wasn't covered in glue," Violet said, beaming at her.

Chapter Seven

Luna edged carefully off the window frame and on to the roof below, padding cautiously across the sloping surface. This was much more exciting to explore than the boxes under the bed. The clay tiles made it quite easy to grip, although they felt rough on her soft paws. Luna zigzagged up and down and stepped over on to a different part of the roof. It seemed to turn a corner, pointing further out and away from the bedroom window. But if she looked round she could still see the open window behind her, ready to go back whenever she wanted.

Another bee zoomed past, and she hopped quickly after it and skidded a little. It was only a tiny slip, but Luna flattened down against the tiles at once, clinging on as tight as she could. Her heart was thumping inside her – that had been close! She had to be more careful.

It was getting colder too, she thought with a shiver. The bright sun had gone in and the blue of the sky was fading to a whitish-grey. Luna twitched in surprise as a raindrop splattered against the tiles next to her, and then another one, and then one on her nose. She clung to the roof, looking worriedly around as the rain splashed down. The reddish-brown tiles were darkening now and the water was starting to run into the gutters. She huddled herself just under the roof ridge, the heavy rain plastering her fur flat against her body.

Luna let out a tiny mew – she didn't want to call too loudly, she felt as if the slightest movement could make her paws slip again. Quietly, cautiously, she cried for her mother and for Nadia. She just wanted to go home…

At the school gates Nadia hugged her dad tight and waved goodbye to Violet. Violet grinned at her and gave her a thumbs up, wishing her luck.

"Why does it always tip down at school pick-up time?" Dad said, beckoning Nadia under his umbrella and rolling his eyes.

"Dad, I need to talk to you about something. It's important."

Dad gave her a worried look. "What's wrong? Has something happened?" He glanced back at the school. "Do I need to go and talk to Miss Evans?"

"No, it's about Luna. And Gracie." Nadia took a deep breath. "I think we should keep them."

Dad was silent for a moment. Then he sighed. "You know, I'm finding it hard to imagine my working day without Gracie lying on my desk. She even gave my hand a little headbutt today. First time she's done that. And I'd miss Luna trying to climb my trouser legs so she can dance up and down on the keyboard."

Nadia squeezed his hand tight. "So … you think we should keep them too?"

He smiled down at Nadia. "Let's see what your mum says."

Nadia let go of Dad's hand and wrapped both her arms round his arm instead, hugging it tight as they walked. Dad loved Gracie and Luna too! They might, just *might*, be able to keep them!

When they got home, Nadia dashed upstairs to find Luna – it was what she usually did straight after school, but today it seemed even more important. She wanted to tell Luna the news.

She hurried into her room, expecting to find Luna curled up on her duvet, or on the squishy cat bed she still shared with Gracie inside the wardrobe. But there was no kitten waiting excitedly for her – and Gracie wasn't there either.

"I hope Dad didn't leave his office door open again," Nadia muttered. The other day when he'd gone to get a cup of tea, Luna had added some very strange figures to a set of accounts he'd been working on.

Dad's office door was closed, though. Nadia stood in the hallway for a moment, feeling confused. Then she heard a worried-sounding mew from the end of the landing.

Gracie was standing by the door to the stairs that led up to Mum and Dad's room in the loft. As Nadia watched, the cat stood up on her hind paws and scrabbled anxiously at the door. Then she looked round at Nadia and meowed loudly.

"Did Luna get in there?" Nadia asked uncertainly. "But … the door's closed." Gracie meowed again, even louder, and this time her paws thudded wildly against the door.

"OK…" Nadia reached out for the door handle and Gracie backed up at once, as though she understood that she needed to be out of the way of the opening door. As soon as Nadia pulled it open, Gracie shot up the stairs, and Nadia dashed after her.

"She isn't here, Gracie," Nadia murmured, looking round her parents' room. "I reckon she must be downstairs somewhere, come on. We'll go and look."

But Gracie wasn't listening. She made a huge leap from the floor up on to the shelving unit just under the window. The *open* window!

"Oh! Gracie, no! You can't go out there." Nadia flung herself after Gracie, who was standing with her front paws up against the window frame, peering out at the roof. Gracie didn't like to be touched, but Nadia thought it would be worse to let her out on to the roof than to grab her. "You mustn't!" she gasped, seizing Gracie just under her front paws and pulling her back. She was trying to be gentle, but Gracie was so wriggly, desperately clinging on to the window.

Then, from outside, there came a tiny, frightened mew.

Gracie wriggled even harder and Nadia stood on tiptoe, peering out of the window. Out there on the roof was a hunched, bedraggled ball of wet fur.

"Luna!" Nadia breathed in horror.

She put Gracie on the bed and pulled the window down a bit, so that the open gap was only tiny. She was pretty sure Gracie couldn't squeeze out of that. Then she ran to the top of the loft stairs. "*Dad!* Luna's on the roof!" she yelled. "She's stuck! Help! Dad!" She could hear her dad thundering up the stairs.

"What? How did she even get up here?"

"I don't know!" Nadia wailed. "Come and see. Gracie was trying to get out too, I had to shut the window."

Gracie was back up on the shelving unit now, pacing back and forth and mewing frantically. She looked as if she was desperate to get out.

"That was sensible," Dad murmured.
He pressed his nose against the glass,
trying to see out. "Oh wow… There
she is."

"I think she's stuck," Nadia said
worriedly.

"I don't see why she hasn't just
come back again," Dad said, frowning.
"Unless she got scared when it started

raining, I suppose?"

"What if she falls off?" Nadia whispered.

Dad put his arm round her. "I don't think she will, don't worry. She's a good climber. Cats can get to the most incredible places sometimes." He sighed. "They just aren't always very good at getting back again."

Gracie mewed loudly again, staring at them both, her eyes round with fear.

"We'll get her back," Nadia told the anxious cat. "We will, Dad, won't we?"

"Actually, I've got an idea," Dad said, hurrying to the stairs. "Don't let Gracie get out there, Nadia, I'll be back in a minute."

It felt much longer – Nadia kept pressing herself close to the window, to check on the kitten. It had stopped raining but Luna's fur was still plastered flat all over. She was usually so fluffy but now she seemed scarily tiny.

At last she heard Dad coming back, muttering to himself and banging into things – and then he appeared at the top of the stairs with a long plank of wood. It was one of the pieces left over from building the decking in the garden, Nadia realized.

"What's that for?" Gracie was staring at him in horror and Nadia thought maybe she was too.

"It's a bridge," Dad said, trying to move round the bed to get the plank lined up with the window. "I think Luna's too scared to walk back round the corner of that wet roof. So if I rest this on the tiles, just next to her, she can go straight across instead."

"Oh…" Nadia smiled hopefully. "That's brilliant!"

"You need to stop Gracie trying to get out of the window when I open it," Dad explained. "Actually, maybe we'd better put her downstairs?"

Nadia looked at Gracie and Gracie looked back. Every hair of her said that she wasn't going anywhere.

Dad sighed. "Maybe not. OK. We're doing our best, you know," he murmured to Gracie. "Stay there." Carefully, he opened the window a little more and slid the piece of wood out. "I hope it's long enough… Yes! There we go. Now we just have to hope Luna understands what she's supposed to do…"

Chapter Eight

Luna gave a tiny mew of fright as the piece of wood came lumbering towards her out of the window. It clunked against the roof tiles and she felt them shudder. What was happening? She could see Nadia's dad in the window, but she had no idea what he was trying to do and she was too frightened to work it out. She froze in place and closed her eyes tightly. Where was Nadia? Where was her mother? She was so cold and so scared, and so desperate to be home… Everything seemed to be frozen. She couldn't make herself move and she couldn't make herself think, either. She could only sit still, and wait, and hope.

"Is Luna coming?" Nadia demanded, squashing up close to Dad. It was hard to see round his shoulder with the shelving unit in the way.

"No… Not yet," her dad said doubtfully. "I'm not sure she understands what we're trying to do – I thought she'd see it was a bridge, but maybe it just looks like a big, scary thing to her."

Nadia stood on tiptoe and then caught her breath at the sight of Luna. The piece of wood next to her made her look even smaller. She had her eyes closed, as though she was trying to shut everything out.

"It's not working," she said, her voice going high and frightened. What if they couldn't get Luna back in? She didn't want to think about it, but she couldn't stop…

"I'm going to go and see if Pete's home next door. He's got a ladder," Dad muttered. "I'll be back in a minute, Nadia. Don't let Gracie escape, OK? And don't lean out, it's not safe."

"All right," Nadia whispered. She wasn't absolutely sure she could stop Gracie, though. The window was only open enough for the decking plank to fit through, but it was a fat piece of wood and Gracie was quite a skinny cat.

Maybe we ought to let her try? Nadia wondered, eyeing the anxious-looking tabby pacing the shelves. She'd seen

Gracie pick up her kittens in her mouth, although she hadn't done it in a little while. Was Luna too big to carry now? Nadia shuddered at the thought of Gracie walking back along that plank bridge, with Luna dangling from her mouth. No, that was *not* a good idea.

Nadia looked out at Luna again. The ginger kitten's fur was still wet enough to be autumn-leaf dark and Nadia was pretty sure that she was shivering. They had to do something soon...

Gracie couldn't carry Luna back, no... But perhaps she and Nadia together could persuade Luna to try for herself.

"Look..." Nadia tapped at the window frame and Gracie gave her an alert, anxious glance. "She's out there.

We have to get her back again. We have to get her home. Come on, Gracie. Call her," she pleaded. "I wish I could make you understand." She looked out again. "Oh, her eyes are open!"

Luna looked a tiny bit less like a statue kitten – she was staring at the window now.

"Oh, ow!" Nadia squeaked, as Gracie clawed her way up beside her, scrabbling at the edge of the window and practically hanging from her front paws. Gracie meowed loudly and Nadia saw Luna's ears flicker. She'd *definitely* heard that.

"Yes, yes, Luna, come on…" she called – not too loud, she mustn't scare her. Ever so slowly, Luna eased out of her terrified crouch, wobbling on to

114

her little white paws and eyeing them
nervously.

Gracie mewed again, and wriggled,
and Nadia had to grab her. She really
didn't want two cats out on the roof.
In the panic, the two of them almost
missed Luna stepping cautiously on to
the plank of wood.

Luna could see them both, her mother
and Nadia calling to her. They sounded
scared, and that frightened Luna – but
it made her want to be back with them
more. Nadia was home. Nadia had fed
her and cared for her, she made Luna
think of curling up asleep together, of
gentle strokes and delicious food and

all those bottles of milk…

They were just there, only a short distance away. The plank of wood actually looked quite wide and flat now, quite safe. She stood up shakily and set her paw on to the fragile bridge. It didn't give at all and the tiny kitten started to pad across. She could see the blur of a striped face and Nadia's dark, worried eyes ahead.

"You're doing it! Well done, Luna! I'll open the window a bit more." There was a scuffle and Luna saw her mother's white whiskers flutter as she suddenly disappeared from the open crack of window. Then she froze, huddling down against the plank as the window creaked opened wider. Her bridge shook a little, but she saw Nadia again and heard her call softly, "It's all right! Come on, you can get all the way in now, come on, Luna…"

The kitten paced daintily to the edge of the window. She hesitated at the end of the wooden plank, unsure about the drop down, but then she felt Nadia's hands close gently around her. She was lifted and immediately tucked close against Nadia's T-shirt. She could feel her hands shaking.

"Nadia, you've got her!"

Nadia looked up in surprise to see

her mum at the bedroom door. She was sitting on the edge of her mum and dad's bed, with Luna cuddled against her and Gracie standing half on her lap, nosing against her fingers. Slowly, she put Luna down on the bedcover so that Gracie could sniff her over properly.

"I didn't know you were home," she said, standing up to hug her mum.

"I just got back from work – I met your dad coming from Pete's with a ladder. Oh! Wait a minute." She stepped over to the window and called, "Rafi! It's all right, Nadia's got her. Put that ladder down!" Then she glanced at Gracie and Luna. "Shall we take them downstairs? I want to get them both away from that window. It worked then?" she added, as Nadia picked up Luna, and Gracie followed them down the stairs.

"Gracie and I called her," Nadia explained. "Oh, Mum, I was so scared she was going to fall off the roof."

Mum shivered. "When your dad told me what had happened, I had a horrible feeling I was going to get up there and find you out on the roof with her. Let's go into your room, I expect it's where Gracie and Luna both feel safest. We can get a towel to dry her off too, she's soaked."

Nadia sat down on her bed and Gracie leaped up beside her to nuzzle at Luna. Her own mum was doing the same thing, Nadia realized, smiling a little as Mum sat down on the bed too and put an arm round her and helped her to rub Luna dry.

After a while, Luna wriggled out
of the towel and sat in the middle of
the duvet with her eyes closed, while
Gracie licked her ears thoroughly.
Luna looked as though she wasn't
happy about it, but she knew it
wouldn't be a good idea to try and run
away.

"Pete took the ladder back," Nadia's
dad said, as he came into the room and

collapsed on the beanbag chair. "I've got to admit, I'm glad I didn't have to climb up it, even with him holding on to it for me. It looked a bit shaky."

"I don't want any of you up ladders, or wandering around rooves," Nadia's mum said with a shudder, watching Luna hunch up as Gracie went on washing her. "I'm so glad you got her back safely, Nadia, I couldn't bear it if anything had happened to her. It made me think – it's going to be so hard to say goodbye." She looked over at Nadia's dad and sighed.

"What if we kept her, Mum?" Nadia burst out. "Kept both of them? They love each other so much. It was Gracie who knew where Luna was. She was scratching at the door to the stairs."

"Definitely both of them," Dad said. "I know you had to persuade me about the fostering when we started, Farida, but I don't want to give them back either now." He leaned over and stretched out his hand to Gracie. The tabby cat eyed him for a moment, then she stopped licking Luna and licked Dad's hand instead. Luna grabbed her chance, scooting away to climb into Nadia's lap.

Mum laughed. "I never expected your dad would fall in love with a cat, Nadia. I was definitely right about you, though…"

Nadia looked between them anxiously. "So … Mum … can we?"

"Yes." Mum reached out to rub Luna's damp ears. "Yes, let's keep them. I know Michelle hoped we might foster another mum about to have kittens, but actually we might have found her another fosterer instead. Your nani said she was going to call Michelle. She misses Milo so much, but she's not ready for another cat of her own just yet, and she'd like to try fostering."

"Nani would be brilliant!" Nadia said, nodding eagerly.

"You know what we are?" Mum said, shaking her head. "There's a name for it, Michelle told me. Failed fosterers. That's when you're only supposed to be fostering a pet for a few weeks and you end up keeping them."

Dad shook his head. "I don't think we failed! These two are going to have a forever home, aren't they? A home with people who already love them."

"Forever, Luna. Did you hear that?" Nadia whispered to the kitten, as she stomped her paws up and down and then collapsed into a sleepy ball on Nadia's legs.

Luna let out a soft, wheezy kitten snore. Or perhaps a purr. Forever was good.

Out Now

From MULTI-MILLION best-selling author
Holly Webb

The Kitten Next Door

Illustrated by Sophy Williams

Out Now

From MULTI-MILLION best-selling author

Holly Webb

The Puppy Who Ran Away

Illustrated by Sophy Williams

HOLLY WEBB

Holly Webb started out as a children's book editor and wrote her first series for the publisher she worked for. She has been writing ever since, with over one hundred books to her name. Holly lives in Berkshire, with her husband and three children. Holly's pet cats are always nosying around when she is trying to type on her laptop.

For more information about Holly Webb visit:

www.holly-webb.com